FINGERPRINTS *on the* TABLE
THE STORY OF THE WHITE HOUSE TREATY TABLE

THE WHITE HOUSE HISTORICAL ASSOCIATION

is a nonprofit organization, chartered on November 3, 1961,
to enhance understanding, appreciation, and enjoyment of the historic
White House. Income from the sale of the association's books and guides
is returned to the publications program and is used as well to acquire
historical furnishings and memorabilia for the White House.

This book has been brought to publication through the generous
assistance of the Hon. Walter H. Annenberg White House Publications Fund.

White House Historical Association
740 Jackson Place, N.W.
Washington, D.C. 20006
www.whitehousehistory.org

President: Neil W. Horstman

PUBLICATIONS
Vice President for Publications, Marcia Mallet Anderson
Production Manager, Books and Special Projects, Abby Clouse-Radigan
Editorial Consultant, Ann Hofstra Grogg
Prepress, Peake-Delancey, Cheverly, Maryland

EDUCATION
Vice President for Education and Scholarship Programs, John Riley
Education Programs Manager, Courtney L. Speaker
Education Programs Assistant Manager, Kathleen A. Munn

1st Edition
9 8 7 6 5 4 3 2 1

ISBN 978-1-931917-14-8

FINGERPRINTS *on the* TABLE
THE STORY OF THE WHITE HOUSE TREATY TABLE

by Connie Remlinger Trounstine
Illustrated by Kerry P. Talbott

WHITE HOUSE HISTORICAL ASSOCIATION
Washington, D.C.

Upstairs in the White House there is a long TABLE . . .

The FINGERPRINTS *of all who touch it are part of its story . . .*

THE STORY BEGINS in 1869, when PRESIDENT ULYSSES S. GRANT ordered a "table for 8 persons" for use in the White House, where presidents live and work.

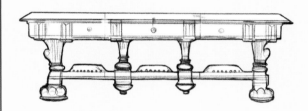

President Grant lived in the White House with his wife Julia and three of their four children: Buck, Nellie, and Jesse. So, why did he order a table for *eight*? That would be too big for his family.

THIS WAS NOT TO BE a dining table, but a conference table where the president would meet with his seven advisers, who together were called his "cabinet."

EACH CABINET MEMBER would have his own place at the new table. Each would have his own drawer with its own lock, and each lock would have its own key.

THE TABLE was to be made of wood from walnut trees that had grown strong and tall for years and years.

LUMBERJACKS cut the trees down. Sawyers cut the trees into planks, and then stacked the lumber on a horse-drawn wagon bound for a factory in New York City.

WAITING AT THE FACTORY were carpenters and cabinetmakers. They had come to New York with toolboxes and dreams.

DID THEY EVER DREAM of making a grand table for the president of the United States?

THERE WAS NO ELECTRICITY at that time. There were no power tools in their workshop. These men depended on their strength and the light of day.

THEY USED MANY SAWS AND CHISELS to remove chunks of wood and to carve the table's giant legs. They worked with their hands, and they left their fingerprints on the table.

WHEN THEY FINISHED THE TABLE, one of the men celebrated by putting his strong hands on his workbench, throwing all his weight above him . . . balancing himself on two hands . . . then on one hand. With his other hand he waved to his fellow workers. And they waved back.

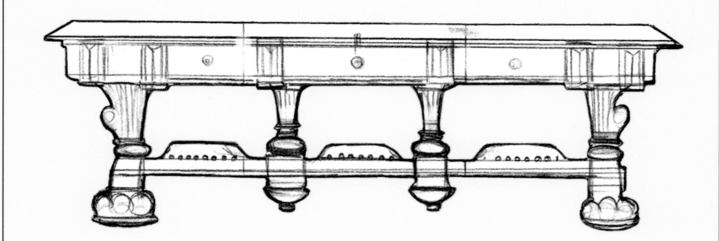

THEN THE WORKERS WALKED TO THE TRAIN STATION, where they watched ten strong men place the crate holding the walnut table into a boxcar. An engineer drove the freight train from New York to Washington, D.C., . . .

where PRESIDENT GRANT was waiting.

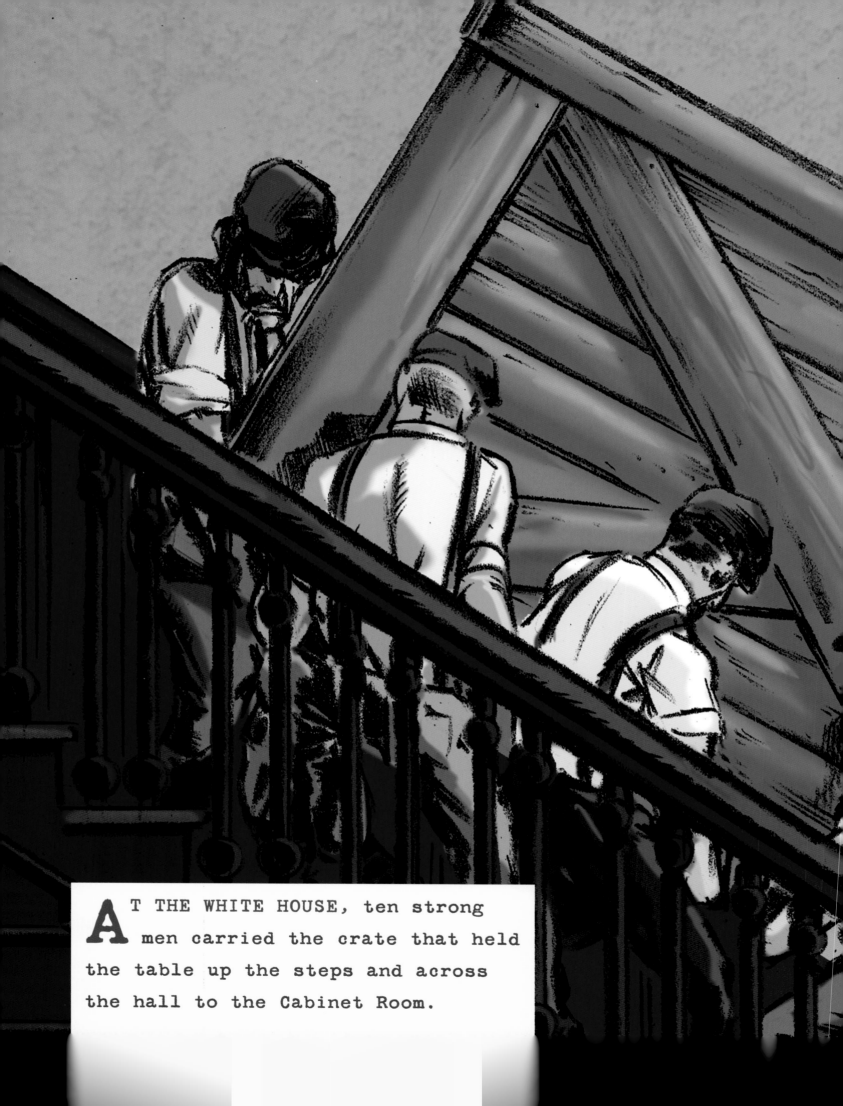

AT THE WHITE HOUSE, ten strong men carried the crate that held the table up the steps and across the hall to the Cabinet Room.

PRESIDENT GRANT SOON MET with his
seven advisers—the cabinet members—
in the Cabinet Room. Each had his own
place at the table and his own drawer
to keep important papers. The cabinet
members were able to lock their own
drawers and keep their papers safe.

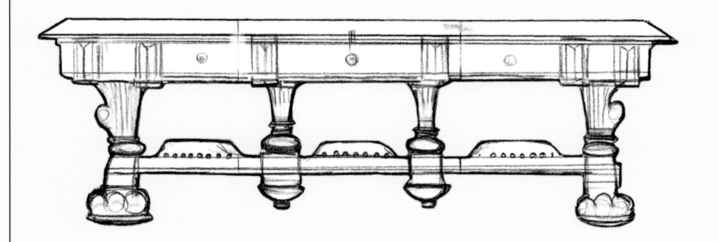

DID PRESIDENT GRANT'S CHILDREN ever
sneak into the Cabinet Room? Did
they jiggle the drawers to see if they
would open?

FOR MANY YEARS, the presidents of the United States and their families moved in and out of the White House while the table remained in the same room on the Second Floor. During those years, the presidents often met at the table with their cabinet members to make important decisions.

FROM THE ROOM, THE TABLE WAS A WITNESS to the lives of the presidents and their families. The table was in the Cabinet Room when the Grants left the White House and PRESIDENT RUTHERFORD B. HAYES moved in with his family.

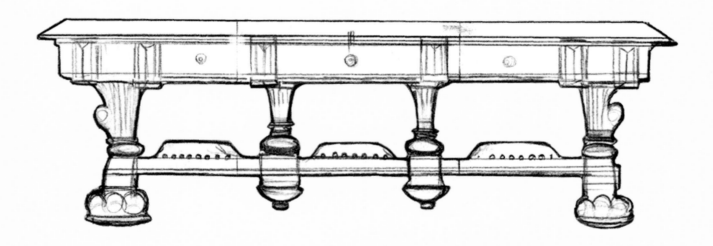

SCOTT HAYES, the president's son, came up with the idea of an Easter egg roll on the White House lawn. The first one was in 1879, and the tradition continues today.

THE TABLE WAS IN THE CABINET ROOM when
PRESIDENT GROVER CLEVELAND married
Frances Folsom in 1886. And it was there
when their daughter Esther was born in
the White House in 1893.

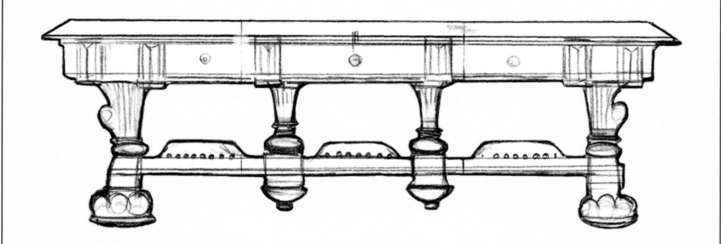

IN 1898, PRESIDENT WILLIAM MCKINLEY stood behind the table in the Cabinet Room when the peace protocol was signed with Spain, ending the Spanish-American War.

SOON AFTER the peace document was signed, newspaper reporters began to call the long walnut table the TREATY TABLE.

THEN CAME A TIME when the TREATY TABLE just didn't work for the president anymore. His cabinet had grown from seven to nine advisers. Also, when PRESIDENT THEODORE ROOSEVELT, his wife, and six children moved into the White House in 1901, there was not enough room on the Second Floor for all the family and all the advisers.

So the West Wing of the White House was built for the president's office, with a new Cabinet Room and an even longer cabinet table.

IN 1929, PRESIDENT CALVIN COOLIDGE asked ten strong men to carry the TREATY TABLE to the East Room, the biggest and grandest room in the White House. There he signed a peace treaty with fourteen other nations, promising not to use war to settle disagreements. It was called the Pact of Paris.

In 1936 the TREATY TABLE was moved to the Ground Floor, some distance away from presidents, presidents' children, and all of their fingerprints.

IN 1961, PRESIDENT JOHN F. KENNEDY and his family moved into the White House. First Lady Jacqueline Kennedy loved learning about the history of the White House. She discovered the TREATY TABLE on the Ground Floor and decided to return it to the place in the room where President Grant's cabinet once met. In its honor, the Cabinet Room was renamed the Treaty Room.

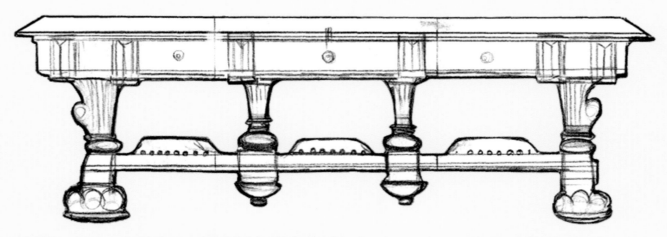

DID PRESIDENT KENNEDY'S children—Caroline and John Jr.—ever sneak into the Treaty Room? Did they jiggle the drawers to see if they would open? Did they leave fingerprints on the table?

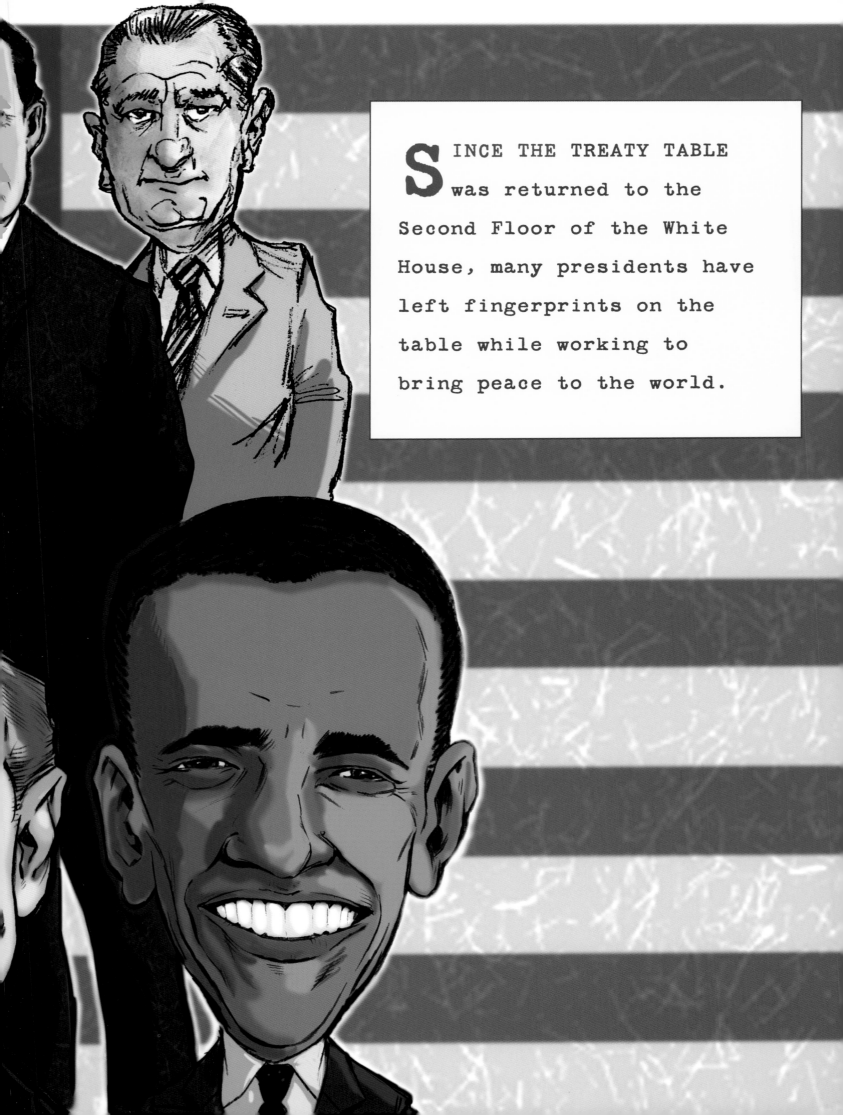

SINCE THE TREATY TABLE was returned to the Second Floor of the White House, many presidents have left fingerprints on the table while working to bring peace to the world.

AS NEW TREATIES ARE SIGNED to encourage peace, many more fingerprints will find their way onto the table. Touched by carpenters, children, and world leaders, the TREATY TABLE continues to witness moments of peacemaking from its home in the White House.

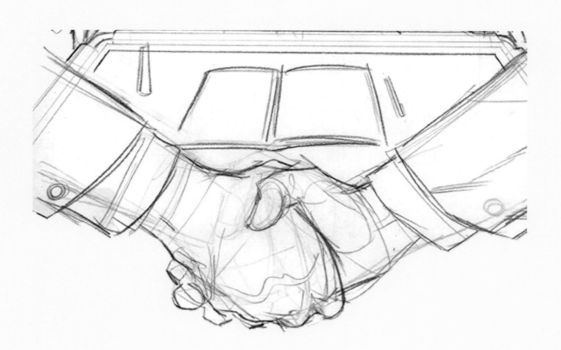

Publisher's Note

This book is inspired by the Treaty Table, a real object that remains in the White House collection today. Much of our story is set in the White House at 1600 Pennsylvania Avenue in Washington, D.C., and centers on actual historical events and real people, including the presidents and their families. The workers are fictional characters created to reflect the facts known about carpentry and the New York furniture trade in the mid-nineteenth century. As this is a fictional account of events that were not recorded, we have taken some artistic license in portraying scenes of the making and delivery of the table, but we have not deviated in any significant ways from known history.

Sources

HERTER BROTHERS: FURNITURE AND INTERIORS FOR A GILDED AGE, by Katherine S. Howe, Alice Cooney Frelinghuysen, and Catherine Hoover Voorsanger (New York: Abrams, 1994). See the chapter entitled "From the Bowery to Broadway: The Herter Brothers and the New York Furniture Trade."

"PEACEFUL END TO MIDEAST NEGOTIATIONS," by Terence Hunt, Associated Press, October, 24, 1998.

"POTTIER & STYMUS MFG. CO.: ARTISTIC FURNITURE & DECORATIONS," by David A. Hanks, in *Art & Antiques*, September–October 1982: 84–91.

THE PRESIDENTS OF THE UNITED STATES OF AMERICA, by Michael Beschloss (Washington, D.C.: White House Historical Association, 2009). The stories of the lives and administrations of each of the American presidents from George Washington through Barack Obama, illustrated with portraits in the White House collection.

THE WHITE HOUSE: ITS FURNISHINGS AND FIRST FAMILIES, by Betty C. Monkman (New York: Abbeville Press, 2000). Details the 200-year history of the furnishings and decorative objects in the White House collection.

Further Reading

ART IN THE WHITE HOUSE: A NATION'S PRIDE by William Kloss (Washington, D.C.: White House Historical Association, 2007). Features the nearly 500 paintings, sculptures, and drawings in the White House collection.

THE FIRST LADIES OF THE UNITED STATES OF AMERICA by Allida Black (Washington, D.C.: White House Historical Association, 2009). Profiles the many women, from Martha Washington to Michelle Obama, who have maintained the traditions of hospitality in the White House.

THE LIVING WHITE HOUSE by Betty C. Monkman (Washington, D.C.: White House Historical Association, 2007). Presents more than 200 years of the history of White House life with hundreds of pictures of past and present first families, children and pets; workers and daily routines; important State occasions and informal public celebrations.

THE PRESIDENT'S HOUSE by William Seale (Washington, D.C.: White House Historical Association, 2009). A treasury of the people, the plans, and the purposes that have shaped the White House from the very beginning.

THE WHITE HOUSE ABC: A PRESIDENTIAL ALPHABET by John Hutton (Washington, D.C.: White House Historical Association, 2005). A whimsical illustrated alphabet featuring the names of the presidents and words associated with the White House in five languages.

THE WHITE HOUSE: AN HISTORIC GUIDE (Washington, D.C.: White House Historical Association, 2011). The celebrated spaces and rich history of each of the public rooms and many of the private areas of the White House, portrayed in this continually updated guidebook.

THE WHITE HOUSE: THE HISTORY OF AN AMERICAN IDEA by William Seale (Washington, D.C.: White House Historical Association, 2001). A richly illustrated reference that brings together the story of the architecture of the White House with the story of the first families and designers who shaped it.

Presidents and Administrations Referenced in This Story

ULYSSES S. GRANT
18th president, served from 1869 to 1877 (pages 6–9, 19, and 22–25)

RUTHERFORD B. HAYES
19th president, served from 1877 to 1881 (pages 28–29)

GROVER CLEVELAND
22nd and 24th president, served from 1885 to 1889 and from 1893 to 1897 (pages 30–31)

WILLIAM MCKINLEY
25th president, served from 1897 to 1901 (pages 32–33)

THEODORE ROOSEVELT
26th president, served from 1901 to 1909 (pages 34–35)

CALVIN COOLIDGE
30th president, served from 1923 to 1929 (pages 36–37)

JOHN F. KENNEDY
35th president, served from 1961 to 1963 (pages 38–39)

LYNDON B. JOHNSON
36th president, served from 1963 to 1969 (pages 40–41)

RICHARD M. NIXON
37th president, served from 1969 to 1974 (pages 40–41)

GERALD R. FORD
38th president, served from 1974 to 1977 (pages 40–41)

JIMMY CARTER
39th president, served from 1977 to 1981 (pages 40–41)

RONALD REAGAN
40th president, served from 1981 to 1989 (pages 40–41)

GEORGE H. W. BUSH
41st president, served from 1989 to 1993 (pages 40–41)

WILLIAM J. CLINTON
42nd president, served from 1993 to 2001 (pages 40–41)

GEORGE W. BUSH
43rd president, served from 2001 to 2009 (pages 40–41)

BARACK OBAMA
44th president, served from 2009 to present (pages 40–41)

About the Table

THE WHITE HOUSE: ITS FURNISHINGS AND FIRST FAMILIES, by Betty C. Monkman, includes the following detailed curatorial record on the Treaty Table:

CONFERENCE TABLE
Pottier & Stymus Manufacturing Co.
New York, 1869
Walnut / mahogany, tulip poplar; leather
U.S. Government purchase
1869, 869.209.1
28 3/4 x 96 1/2 x 48 in. (73.0 x 245.1 x 121.9 cm)

Marks: None.
Notes: One "table for 8 persons" from a suite of furniture purchased for the Cabinet Room in 1869. Eight locking drawers were available to the president and the seven cabinet officers as of 1869 (State, War, Treasury, Navy, Interior, Attorney General, and Postmaster General). The table continued to be used by the Cabinet until 1902 when a new Cabinet Room was provided in the newly constructed Executive Office Building (West Wing). In 1961, Mrs. Kennedy reassembled the surviving pieces from the suite—this table, the sofa, and four chairs in that same Second Floor room, renamed the Treaty Room, which had served as the Cabinet Room from 1865 to 1902. The historic documents that have been signed on this table include:
1. The Peace Protocol ending hostilities of the Spanish-American War, August 12, 1898, witnessed by President William McKinley in the Cabinet Room.
2. The Pact of Paris (Kellogg-Briand Peace Pact), 1929, signed by President Calvin Coolidge in the East Room.
3. Arms and nuclear testing treaties with the Soviet Union signed in the East Room by Presidents Nixon (1972), Ford (1976), Reagan (1987), and George H.W. Bush (1990).
4. Treaties with former Soviet republics (Russia, Ukraine, Kazakhstan), 1992, signed by President George H.W. Bush in the East Room.
5. Middle East peace documents including: Egyptian-Israeli Peace Treaty, 1979, on the North Lawn, witnessed by President Jimmy Carter; the Israel-Palestinian Declaration of Principles, 1993, on the South Lawn, hosted by President Bill Clinton.
Condition: Remains of call button system at one end. References: NA/MTA acct. 180754, voucher 2.

About the Painting

The painting on page 33 is entitled *Signing of the Peace Protocol Between Spain and the United States, August 12, 1898.* It was painted by Théobald Chartran in 1899, and it belongs to the White House art collection still today.

About the Contributors

CONNIE REMLINGER TROUNSTINE was a reporter for 29 years at the *Kentucky Post*, a Scripps Howard newspaper. Her interest in the White House Treaty Table began in 1998 when she read in an Associated Press article that: "There were cheers and shouts and hand-shakes in the East Room as the leaders signed the agreement on a walnut conference table used for historic occasions, beginning with the signing of the peace accord ending the Spanish-American War" in 1889. This account led her to wonder what stories such an eyewitness to our country's history might tell. Connie lives in Cincinnati, enjoys fly-fishing, and volunteers at the National Underground Railroad Freedom Center. She is the author of the children's book *The Worst Christmas Ever.*

KERRY P. TALBOTT is an award-winning illustrator who has worked for various Media General newspapers for 20 years, most notably the *Richmond News Leader* and *Richmond Times-Dispatch*. Talbott specializes in caricatures and teaches illustration and sequential imagery in the Communication Arts Department at Virginia Commonwealth University. He is based in Richmond, Virginia.

Acknowledgments

With special thanks to artist John Hutton; former White House curator Betty Monkman; White House curator William G. Allman and The Office of the Curator, the White House; and the teachers at Terra Centre Elementary School in Burke, Virginia.